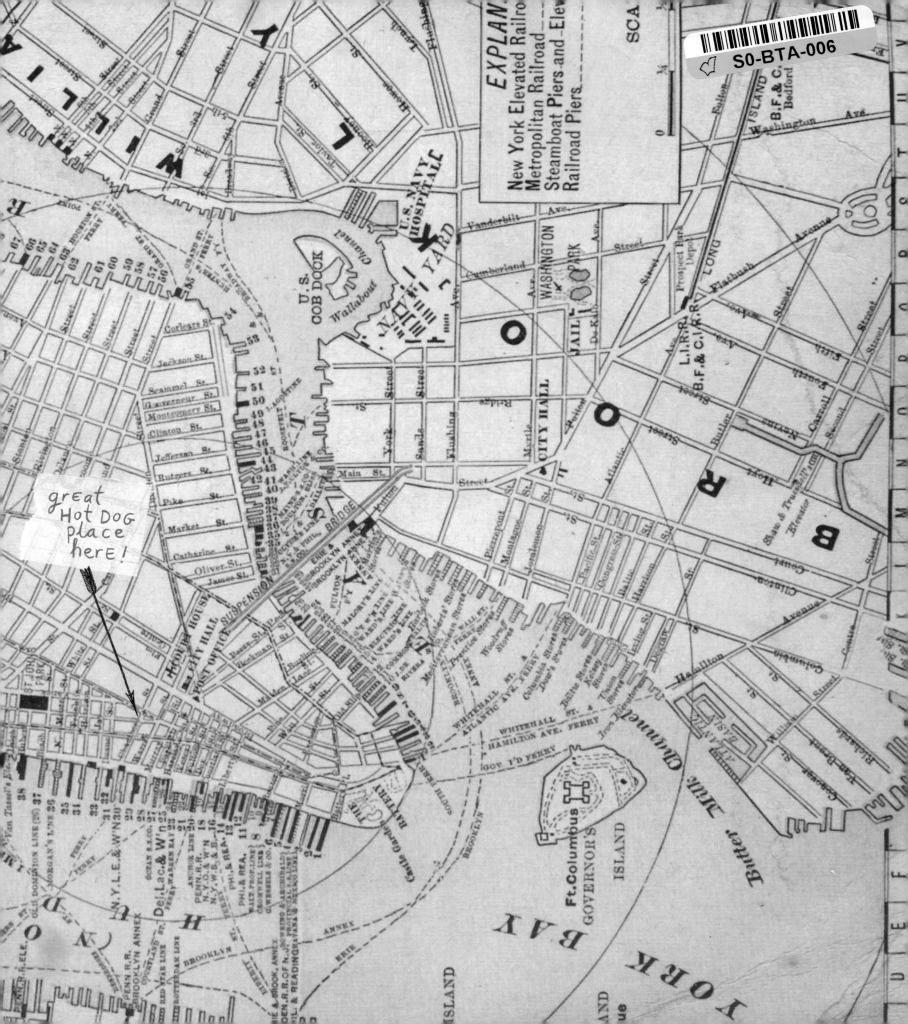

for mum & dad

A Neal Porter Book
published by Roaring Brook Press
Roaring Brook Press is a Division of Holtzbrinck
Publishing holdings LIMITED partnership
175 fifth Avenue, New York, New York 10010
mackids.com

Library of Congress Cataloging-in-Publication data

Gordon, Gus, author, illustrator.
Herman and Rosie/Gus Gordon. — first edition.
pages cm
"a Neal Porter BOOK."
summary: in New York City, a "groovy little jazz number" brings
together a lonely crocodile and deer.
ISBN 978-1-59643-856-9 (hardcover: alk.paper)
[1. Friendship—fiction. 2. Loneliness—Fiction. 3. Jazz—fiction.
4.Crocodiles—fiction.5.deer—fiction.6. new york (N.Y.)—fiction.]
I.Title
PZ7.G6573He 2013
[E]—dc23   2012037557

Roaring Brook Press books may be purchased for business or
promotional use. For information on bulk purchases please
contact Macmillan Corporate and Premium Sales Department at
(800)221-7945 x5442 or by email at specialmarkets@macmillan.com

First edition 2013
printed in China by Macmillan Production (Asia) ltd.,
Kowloon Bay, Hong Kong (supplier code 10)

1 3 5 7 9 10 8 6 4 2

"I have at last, after several MONTHS' experience,
made up my mind that [New York] is a splendid desert
— a domed and steepled solitude, where the stranger is
LONELY in the midst of a million of his race."

Mark Twain, june 5, 1867

gus gordon

HERMAN AND ROSIE

A Neal Porter Book
Roaring Brook Press
New York

Once upon a time in a very busy city,
on a very busy street,
in two very small apartments,
lived Herman Schubert . . .

here

. . . and Rosie Bloom.

Over Here

Herman lived on the seventh floor.

He liked potted plants, playing the oboe,
wild boysenberry yogurt, the smell of hot dogs
in the winter, and watching films about the ocean.

Rosie lived on the fifth floor in the building next door.

She liked pancakes, listening to old jazz records,
the summertime subway breeze, toffees that stuck
to her teeth, singing on the fire escape . . .

and watching films about the ocean.

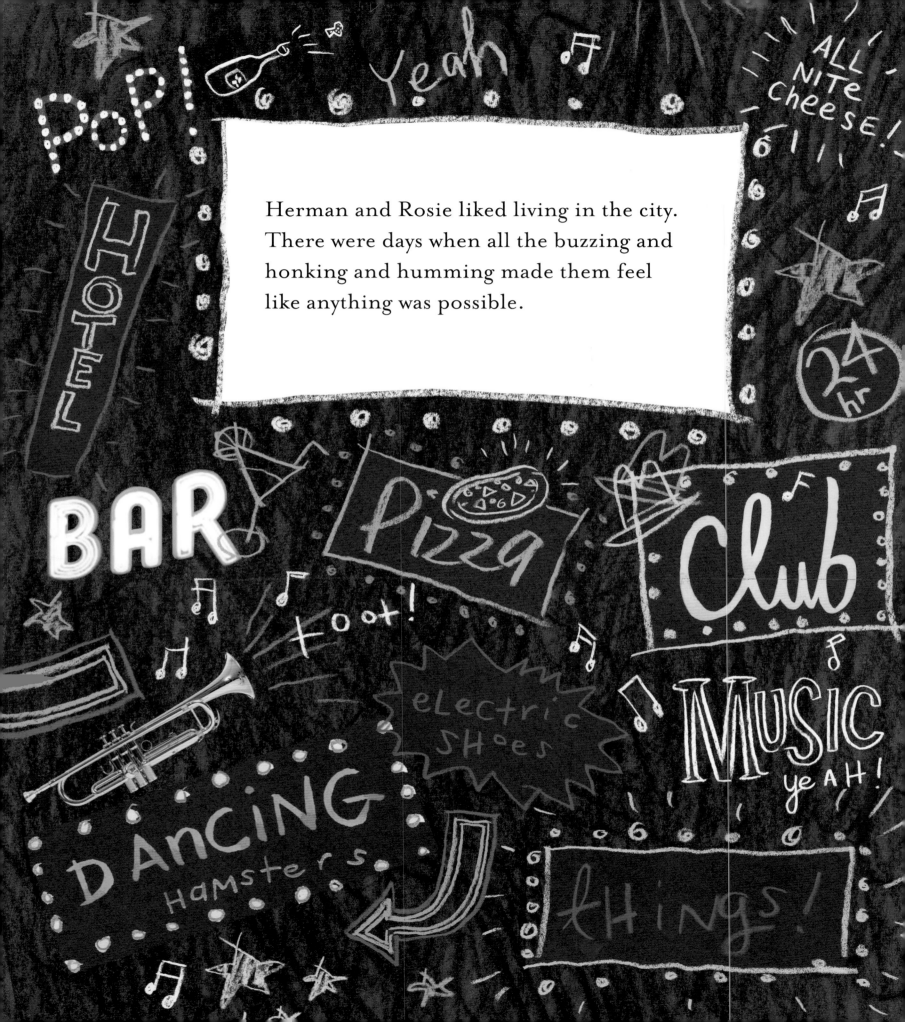

Herman and Rosie liked living in the city.
There were days when all the buzzing and
honking and humming made them feel
like anything was possible.

But often the city was a lonely place.

Herman worked in a tall building in an office on the fifty-first floor. He spent all day on the phone selling things.

Not everyone wanted to buy "a thing." But this didn't matter to Herman. He just loved having someone to talk to.

Rosie worked uptown
in a fine restaurant.

In the afternoons she
rode to singing lessons.

On Thursday nights she sang for two hours at a small downtown jazz club. It was the highlight of her week.

the Mangy Hound jazz club

One day on his way home from work,
Herman heard a noise. It wasn't a normal city noise.
It was a different kind of noise. Someone was singing . . .

Mrs A Schwarzmann's JAZZ acAdemy

. . . and it was wonderful. It made him feel like he had eaten honey straight from the jar.

That night, with the singing in his head,
Herman took his oboe to the roof and played
a groovy little jazz number.

In the building next door, Rosie began to hum and her toes began to tingle. Oboe music filled the room. It was the most splendid sound she had ever heard.

And it stayed in her head (like good tunes do).
She hummed it as often as she could,
so it didn't fade away.

For days it seemed that the music was following them.
Herman kept hearing that beautiful voice and
Rosie kept hearing that groovy tune.

Everywhere.

Then, one morning, Herman arrived at work to find that he had lost his job. He just wasn't selling enough things.

No. 157

herman

The boss

Herman thought he had sold lots of things, but in truth he was so happy to be talking to someone he often forgot about the selling part.

That evening at
the Mangy Hound jazz club,
Rosie sang up a storm.

But there was no one
there to hear it. After her set,
Rosie was given some bad news.
The club was closing down.

Herman left his office for the last time.
He didn't feel like playing his oboe that night.

getouddahere!

beep

tAXi honk

Beep

TaXi honk

hey buddY!

uptown
33rd

and 7th

Honk

downtown

honk

crash

Don't HONK

51st

apples

beep
beep

And Rosie didn't feel like singing.

The city felt busier and
louder and darker than usual.

Herman Schubert sat in his small apartment eating pretzels. To cheer himself up he decided to watch his entire Jacques Cousteau underwater film collection.

Packed away neatly under the bed sat Herman's oboe.

Rosie Bloom stood in the kitchen of her small apartment making pancakes. Lots of pancakes. Way more than she could ever possibly eat.

This didn't make her feel any better, so she sat down and watched her entire Jacques Cousteau underwater film collection.

Days
and nights
and weeks inched by.
Rosie lost her voice to sounds of the city
and Herman lost the urge to play his oboe.

The city kept on moving,
but everything had fallen out of tune.

Then one morning something was different.

Rosie woke suddenly—
she needed toffee that stuck to her teeth!

Herman woke suddenly—he had a craving
for wild boysenberry yogurt!

It was such a beautiful day outside that Herman
soon forgot his yogurt and Rosie forgot her toffee.

Instead, they walked . . .

TRANSPORTATION MAP

OF

NEW YORK

(Elevated Systems)

KEY

HermaN: ----

Rosie: - - -

SCALE.

0   ¼   ½   1 Statute Mile.

and walked . . .

coffee

and walked . . .

and walked . . .

Until they both ended
up at the same place,

where they each had a hot dog.

Then they both walked home.

That night Herman got out his oboe
from under his bed and headed to the roof.
The city seemed pleased to see him.
Even its rattles and honks sounded musical.

Rosie was cooking and feeling
strangely happy when she heard
the familiar sounds of a groovy
little jazz number.

She dropped the frying pan. She just *had* to follow that tune.

Out . . . up . . . and over . . . until . . .

Once upon a time in a very busy city,
on a very busy street,
on top of a very tall building,
Rosie found Herman. And Herman found Rosie.
The city was never quite the same.